FROM THE PUBLISHER

In this volume you will find a collection of popular children's stories illustrated by the prolific Walter Crane. Crane was raised in a family of artists, and was considered to be one of the greatest illustrators of the Victorian era. He was a part of the Arts and Crafts movement, and was a very strong contributor to the world of illustrated children's literature. The stories found herein were published during the late nineteenth century, and while we think of them today as "story books" or "picture books," they were better known at the time as "toy books."

The term "toy book" first appeared in the eighteenth century, when small toys were actually included with the books. As time went on, toys were no longer included, but the idea of the books remained the same. Books were short, often 8–10 pages each, with an emphasis on large, colorful illustrations and minimal text. The text was often classic fairy tales, nursery rhymes, or songs; therefore you would be able to find different versions of the same story done by different publishers and illustrators.

By the time the toy book trend took off in the late 1800s, many different publishers were involved, but the most well-known books were created by the printer Edmund Evans. Evans originally worked with the publisher Routledge and Warne before eventually publishing his own books. He worked with the best-known children's illustrators at the time, and together with Walter Crane, Randolph Caldecott and Kate Greenaway created the most popular children's books of the Victorian era. The style of the books that Evans produced with Crane were even more unique to the time due to Crane's especially bold, colorful, and detailed illustrative style, and the use of text boxes set into the illustrations themselves. This use of text within illustrations is an early version of a graphic novel, and it is also a great way to fully engage the reader with the story.

Victorian toy books set the stage for the story and picture books that we know today. This original collection of illustrated classic stories by Walter Crane is sure to delight the modern reader, both young and old.

THE
WALTER CRANE
STORYBOOK COLLECTION

Walter Crane

Engraved and Printed in Colors by
Edmund Evans

CALLA EDITIONS
Mineola, New York

Bibliographical Note

This Calla edition, first published in 2017, is a new collection of stories, with artwork by Walter Crane, reprinted from the following sources, and originally published between 1865–1876:

"This Little Pig Went to Market" (London: John Lane and Chicago: Stone & Kimball)
"Puss in Boots" (London: George Routledge and Sons)
"Jack and the Bean-stalk" (London and New York: John Lane The Bodley Head)
"The Adventures of Puffy" (London: George Routledge and Sons)
"The Sleeping Beauty" (London and New York: John Lane The Bodley Head)
"Baby's Own Alphabet" (London and New York: John Lane The Bodley Head)
"King Luckie Boy's Party" (London and New York: John Lane and Chicago: Stone & Kimball)
"The Three Bears" (London: George Routledge and Sons)
"Bluebeard" (London and New York: John Lane The Bodley Head)
"Mother Hubbard" (London and New York: John Lane The Bodley Head)
"Valentine and Orson" (London: George Routledge and Sons)
"Cinderella" (London: George Routledge and Sons)

International Standard Book Number

ISBN-13: 978-1-60660-114-3
ISBN-10: 1-60660-114-8

CALLA EDITIONS
An imprint of Dover Publications, Inc.
www.doverpublications.com/calla

Printed in China by RR Donnelley

CONTENTS

·WALTER CRANE'S·
·PICTURE BOOKS·

THIS·LIT:
TLE·PIG
WENT·TO
MARKET

: THIS LITTLE PIG :
WENT TO MARKET

: THIS LITTLE PIG :

WENT TO MARKET

: THIS LITTLE PIG :
: STAYED AT HOME :

THIS
LITTLE
PIG
HAD
ROAST
BEEF

: THIS LITTLE PIG :

: HAD NONE :

: THIS LITTLE PIG :
: CRIED—WEE! WEE!

ALL

THE

WAY

HOME

: HOME :

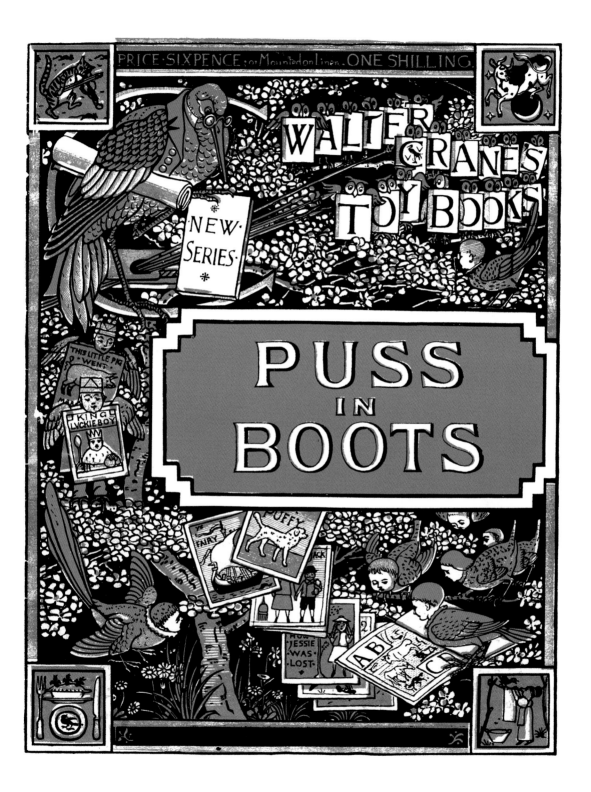

PRICE·SIXPENCE; or Mounted on linen, ONE SHILLING.

WALTER CRANE'S TOY BOOKS

·NEW· ·SERIES·

PUSS IN BOOTS

PUSS IN BOOTS

❖

A MILLER lay dying—he made his last will;
He left his three sons his cat, ass, and mill:
To the eldest the mill, to the second the ass;
The third had the cat, and he cried out, "Alas!
I must starve now, unless I take Puss to eat!"

"No, Master," said Puss, "give me boots to my
feet—
A pair of top-boots—and please leave me alive,
And you shall just see how we'll flourish and
thrive."

So the Puss put on boots, and he started abroad,
And caught a fine rabbit just near the high-road,
Which he took to the palace, and gave to the King:
"This I from the Marquis of Carabas bring."
Again Puss went hunting, and carried the prey
To the King, and the Marquis's duty, each day.

One morn, said the Cat to his Master, "I pray
You to go and to bathe in the river to-day;
The Marquis of Carabas, too, you must be,
And leave all the rest of the business to me."
Now, while the King down by the river passed by,
He heard dismal cries of—"Help! help! or he'll die!
The Marquis of Carabas drowns!—O my Master!"
The King sent his guards to avert the disaster.
The Miller's son finds himself pulled out, and drest
In all that his Majesty had of the best;

And being well dried and well rid of the water,
Was then introduced by the King to his daughter,
And invited to drive in the King's coach-and-four;
And Puss, who had managed all, hurried before,
And seeing men reaping some very fine corn,
Said to them, "You will wish that you'd never been born,
If you don't tell the King, who is now near at hand,
That the Marquis of Carabas owns all this land."
And all whom he met he commanded the same,
To magnify further the Marquis's name.

At last he arrived at a castle so grand,
Which belonged to an Ogre, as well as the land;
Puss conversed with the Ogre, who said that he could
Assume any shape that he chose—bad or good,
Great or small—as he'd show; and the Ogre, so fussy,
Turned into a mouse, and was swallowed by Pussy.
At this moment his Majesty's carriage was heard;
Puss hurried down stairs, and he shortly appeared
At the door, flung wide open before they could ring:
"The Marquis of Carabas welcomes the King!"

19

The Miller's son thus became lord of the place,
And he feasted the King with much grandeur and grace.
After dinner, his Majesty, smiling and bland,
Said, "Marquis of Carabas, give us your hand;
And if there is aught that seems goodly of ours—
Yes, even our daughter—dear Marquis, 'tis yours."
So the Miller's son married the Princess next day,
And Puss was a groomsman, in top-boots so gay;
For the Marquis of Carabas owed him his life—
His lands and his corn-fields—his castle and wife.

20

JACK AND THE BEAN· ·STALK

Jack and the Bean-stalk

IN the days of good King Alfred
  lived a widow with her son;
She was kind, and he was idle, so
  at last their wealth was done,
Nothing left remaining but a cow,
  which must be sold for bread;
Jack, who was to sell, exchanged
  her, and got only beans instead, —
Beans, which when his angry mother
  saw, she flung away in scorn:
Think how great her Jack's surprise
  was, when, on getting up next morn,

23

He perceived the beans had sprouted,—
  grown so very tall and high,
That the topmost of their branches
  seemed to lose itself in sky.
"I must climb," cried Jack, delighted,
  "it seems strong enough to bear;"
When his mother would prevent him,
  no remonstrance would he hear.
Up he goes among the branches,
  easy as a winding stair;
Climbing on for hours, he reaches
  desert lands and bleaker air.
Was no sight or sound to cheer him,
  and he very hungry grew;
As he wandered, sick and weary, an
  old woman came in view;
She was old, her garments tattered,
  and half-blind she seemed, and lame.

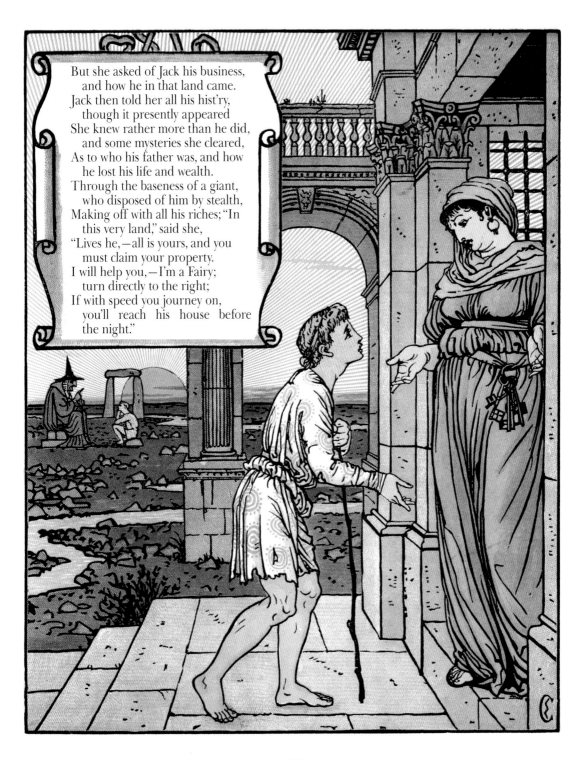

But she asked of Jack his business,
  and how he in that land came.
Jack then told her all his hist'ry,
  though it presently appeared
She knew rather more than he did,
  and some mysteries she cleared,
As to who his father was, and how
  he lost his life and wealth.
Through the baseness of a giant,
  who disposed of him by stealth,
Making off with all his riches; "In
  this very land," said she,
"Lives he,—all is yours, and you
  must claim your property.
I will help you,—I'm a Fairy;
  turn directly to the right;
If with speed you journey on,
  you'll reach his house before
  the night."

On he went, and reached the gi[ant's]
　　　home;
Wife permitted Jack to enter, [and]
Meat and drink she gave [him in the]
　　　house,
And at last she hid him, lest [her]
　　　spouse,
Who, on entering, loudly stated [that]
But was by his wife persua[ded]
(Grieved I am that it consi[sts])
And when he his supper ende[d]
Who a golden egg produ[ced when he said]
　　　"Lay!"
When the giant fell asleep, [Jack]

26

se, and found him not at

so far he'd come;
showed him over all the

pt the hunger of her

lainly smelt fresh meat,
tly his meal to eat,
y of the flesh of men);
brought a splendid hen,
ne'er the giant shouted

d the hen and ran away.

27

Down the bean-stalk home he hastened, and
    upon the magic pelf
Long he lived, his mother also, till at last he
    found himself
Quite inclined for greater riches, as he knew
    an easy road;
Up he climbed the bean-stalk ladder, and
    returned with *such* a load!
But the giant nearly wakened with the barking
    of a dog,—
(Very lucky 'twas for Jack, that way of sleeping
    like a log).

Bags of gold and silver Jack took
  home, but still his mind did lean
Towards another prize, and journey
  up the lucky stalk of bean.
Hidden in his usual corner in the
  giant's house, he spied,
Bought for that great man's amusement,
  playing sweetly by his side
While he slept, a golden harp, which
  Jack at once caught up, and ran,
But the harp with human voice cried,
  "Master, master, stop this man!"
But so tipsy was the giant, though
  he tried to run and bawl,
That, with all his pains, he could not
  stop the flight of Jack at all.

29

Down the road and down the bean-
stalk swiftly ran and clambered
Jack,
Joy was in his manly bosom, and
the harp upon his back.
Down the giant scrambles after
Jack, but little does *he* reck,—
With an axe he cuts the bean-
stalk, and the giant breaks his
neck.
After this, I need not tell you,
Jack resolved to settle down,
Stay at home, climb no more bean-
stalks, be respected in the town.

THE ADVENTURES OF
: PUFFY :

ABOUT a pretty dog I have to tell,—
   A Maltese dog, so curly, white and fluffy;
His nose was pinker than a pink sea-shell,
His eyes were also pink,—his name was PUFFY.
When he was six weeks old, quite small
      and scared,
He came into the house of his new Missis;

His teeth were sharp, he bit so very hard,
She cried, "Oh, what a charming doggie
      this is!"
When Puffy slept he rolled himself up tight,
And looked just like a little worsted bundle;
He used a large round stool to roll and bite,
Which on the floor his Missis used to trundle.

BUT once the little thing fell off a chair,
  And put his shoulder out with that
    sad tumble;
The doctor set and bound it up with care,
While Puffy looked so very wan and humble.
One day he ran out in the street to play
With little friends (his Missis, who will warn her!)

He strays too far,—at last is borne away
By a bad man who lived just round the corner
To his poor Missis none can comfort say,
Her grief by sighs and tears so plainly
    marking;
When he'd been gone a twelvemonth and a day;
Outside the door was heard familiar barking.

AND when the door was opened in there came
Puffy, the worse for wear, and rather shabby,
But plainly the same dog,—a little lame,
And recognised by his old friend the tabby.
How glad his Missis was! and scarce believed
Her eyes that saw her Puffy back returning;

Such scrub and tug his curly back received
For Puffy's was a coat not meant for turning.
So many knots and tangles had his hair,
And such a tedious task it was to comb him,
They took the scissors, and they sheared with care
His little back, that they might better groom him.

35

THIS did not make him look so well,—more lame
    He seemed, indeed he looked a great deal thinner;
"He might be taken for a scrubby lamb,"
They said, "and killed and eaten for our dinner."
Or like a pig he seemed, with curly tail,
Or made one think of an heraldic lion
Upon the shield of some tall knight in mail,
Who treads the stage he shortly means to die on.

A few days after this,—and oh! it shows
   How fickle can be even a kind Missis,—
She grew quite tired of him, as I suppose,
And sent the dear away with many kisses.
His new home in the country he admired,
And was as happy there as may be,
For when of chasing poultry he was tired,
He ate the fiddle-strings and bit the baby.

ONE day in winter, frosty and severe,
   Upon the icy Highgate pond he trotted;
The wind blew sharply, and the air was clear,
And every pond was with its skaters dotted;
And though there was a board marked "DANGEROUS,"
Puffy went running faster, never heeding,
And so fell in,—which shows to all of us
What harm may come if we neglect our reading.

THAT he was drowned my readers must not think,
    For he was dragged with sticks out of his danger
By faithful friends, who, standing on the brink,
    Saw his sad fall, as well as many a stranger.
Half-drowned the poor small thing was, sad to tell,—
    They quickly got some brandy, and he drank it.

THEY took him home, and warmed and rubbed him well,
  And wrapped him carefully in softest blanket.
So he got well;—his equal can't be found,
No pen can e'er describe, no pencil draw him;
And at this moment he is safe and sound,
At least, he was all right when last I saw him.

40

WALTER·CRANE'S·PICTURE·BOOKS·

·THE·SLEEPING·BEAUTY·

THE SLEEPING BEAUTY

L ONG, long ago, in ancient times, there lived a King and Queen,
  And for the blessing of a child their longing sore had been;
At last, a little daughter fair, to their great joy, was given,
And to the christening feast they made, they bade the Fairies seven—

The Fairies seven, who loved the land—that they the child might bless;
Yet one old Fairy they left out, in pure forgetfulness,
And at the feast, the dishes fair were of the reddest gold;
But when the Fairy came, not one for her, so bad and old.
Angry was she, because her place and dish had been forgot,
And angry things she muttered long, and kept her anger hot,

44

Until the Fairy godmothers their gifts and wishes gave:
She waited long to spoil the gifts, and her revenge to have.
One gave the Princess goodness, and one gave her beauty rare;
One gave her sweetest singing voice; one, gracious mien and air;
One, skill in dancing; one, all cleverness; and then the crone
Came forth, and muttered, angry still, and good gift gave she none;

But said, that in the future years the Princess young should die,
By pricking of a spindle-point—ah, woeful prophecy!
But now, a kind young Fairy, who had waited to the last,
Stepped forth, and said, "No, she shall sleep till a hundred years are past;
"And then she shall be wakened by a King's son—truth I tell—
"And he will take her for his wife, and all will yet be well."

In vain in all her fa
In vain in all the country
For in a lonely turret
There lives an ancient wo
The Princess found he
Alas! the spindle pricke

t the spinning-wheel's forbid
pindles sharp are hid;
p a winding stair,
till turns her wheel with care.
lay, and tried to learn to spin;
—the charm had entered in!

And down she falls in death-like sleep: they lay her on her bed,
And all around her sink to rest—a palace of the dead!
A hundred years pass—still they sleep, and all around the place
A wood of thorns has risen up—no path a man can trace.
At last, a King's son, in the hunt, asked how long it had stood,
And what old towers were those he saw above the ancient wood,

An aged peasant told of an enchanted palace, where
A sleeping King and Court lay hid, and sleeping Princess fair,
Through the thick wood, that gave him way, and past the thorns that drew
Their sharpest points another way, the King's son presses through.
He reached the guard, the court, the hall,—and there, where'er he stept,
He saw the sentinels, and grooms, and courtiers as they slept.

Ladies in act to smile, and pages in attendance wait;
The horses slept within their stalls, the dogs about the gate.
The King's son presses on, into an inner chamber fair,
And sees, laid on a silken bed, a lovely lady there;
So sweet a face, so fair—was never beauty such as this;
He stands—he stoops to gaze—he kneels—he wakes her with a kiss.

49

He leads her forth; the magic sleep of all the Court is o'er,—
They wake, they move, they talk, they laugh, just as they did of yore
A hundred years ago. The King and Queen awake, and tell
How all has happed, rejoicing much that all has ended well.
They hold the wedding that same day, with mirth and feasting good—
The wedding of the Prince and Sleeping Beauty in the Wood.

50

WALTER·CRANE'S·PICTURE·BOOKS·

·THE·BABY'S·OWN·

·ALPHABET·

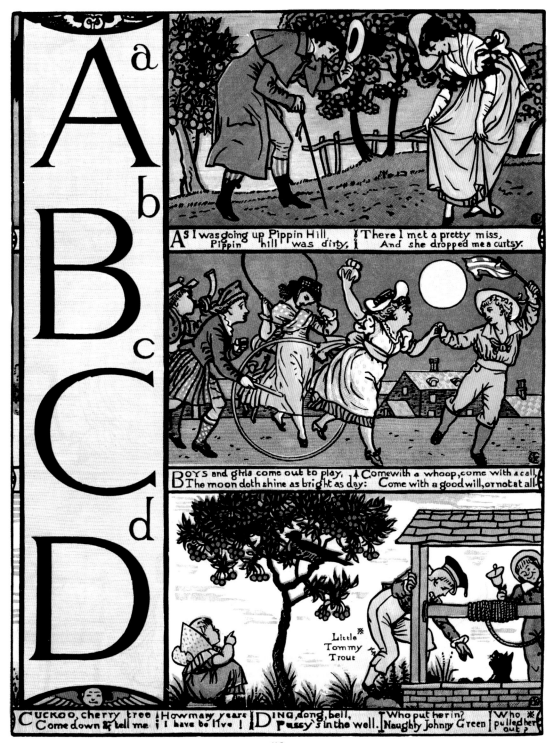

As I was going up Pippin Hill,   There I met a pretty miss,
Pippin hill was dirty,   And she dropped me a curtsy.

Boys and girls come out to play,   Come with a whoop, come with a call,
The moon doth shine as bright as day: Come with a good will, or not at all.

Cuckoo, cherry tree | How many years | Ding dong, bell, | Who put her in? | Who
Come down & tell me | I have to live? | Pussy's in the well. | Naughty Johnny Green | pulled her out?

Little Tommy Trout

EARLY to bed, and early Is the way to be healthy,
to rise, wealthy, and wise.

FOR every evil under the sun If there be one, try and find it;
There is a remedy, or there is none. If there be none, never mind it.

GREAT A, little A; Bouncing B; The cat's in the cupboard, And she can't see me.

54

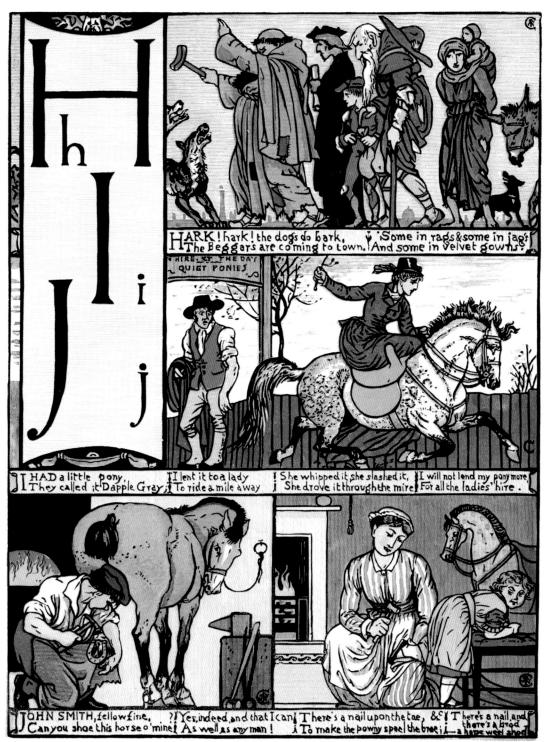

HARK! hark! the dogs do bark,
The Beggars are coming to town.
Some in rags & some in jags,
And some in velvet gowns.

I HAD a little pony,
They called it Dapple Gray;
I lent it to a lady
To ride a mile away
She whipped it, she slashed it,
She drove it through the mire;
I will not lend my pony more,
For all the ladies' hire.

JOHN SMITH, fellow fine,
Can you shoe this horse o' mine?
Yes, indeed, and that I can,
As well as any man!
There's a nail upon the tae,
To make the powny speel the brae;
There's a nail and
there's a brod,
a horse weel shod!

55

KING O'KATCHEM met a king, Says this king to that king
In a narrow lane; "Where have you been?

"Oh, I've be...
With my do...
Pray lend...
That I ma...

"There's t...
TAKE th...
"What's th...
nam...
I've told y...
-rea...
Pray tell a...

LADYBIRD, ladybird, fly away home, All but one that lies under a stone;
Your house is a-fire, your children all gone; Fly thee home, ladybird, ere it be

MULTIPLICATION is vexation, The Rule of Three it puzzles me,
Division's twice as bad; And Fractions drive me mad!

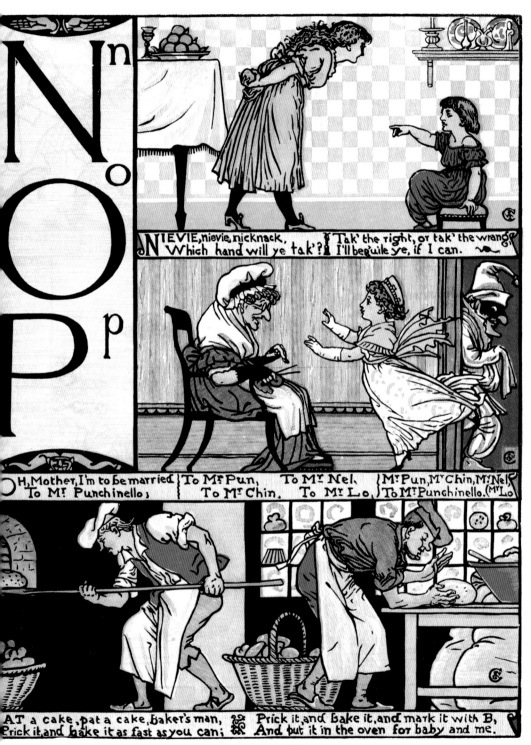

N n
N o
O p
O
P

NIEVIE, nievie, nicknack,   Tak' the right, or tak' the wrange,
Which hand will ye tak'?   I'll beguile ye, if I can.

OH, Mother, I'm to be married   To Mr Pun,   To Mr Nel,   Mr Pun, Mr Chin, Mr Nel,
To Mr Punchinello;   To Mr Chin.   To Mr Lo,   To Mr Punchinello. (Mr Lo

PAT a cake, pat a cake, Baker's man,   Prick it, and bake it, and mark it with B,
Prick it, and bake it as fast as you can;   And put it in the oven for baby and me.

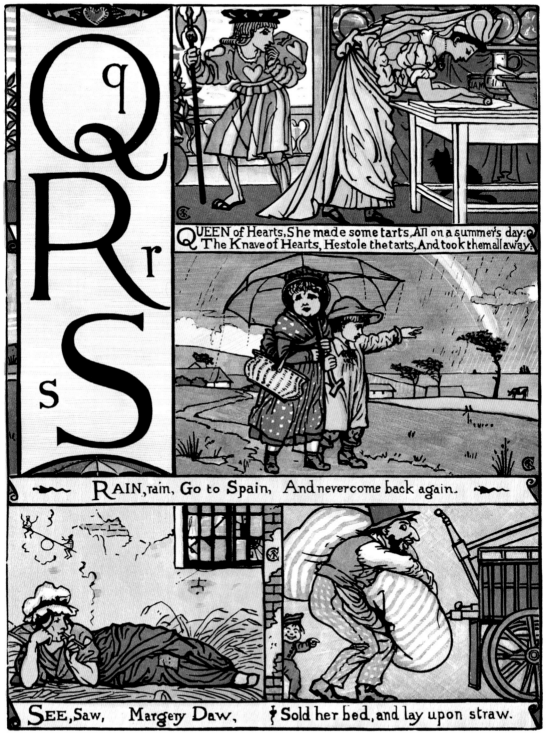

QUEEN of Hearts, She made some tarts, All on a summer's day:
The Knave of Hearts, He stole the tarts, And took them all away:

RAIN, rain, Go to Spain, And never come back again.

SEE, Saw, Margery Daw, Sold her bed, and lay upon straw.

T t

U u

V v

Three children sliding on the ice, As it fell out they all fell in:
Upon a summer's day. The rest they ran away.

UPhill spare me, Down hill ware me, On level ground spare me not, And in the stable forget me not.

VALENTINE The rose is red: the Violets blue The pink is sweet; & so are you.

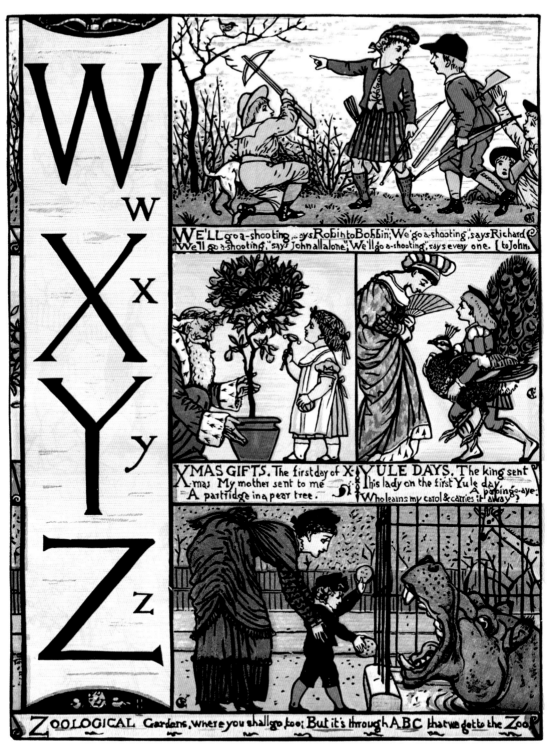

WE'LL go a-shooting, says Robin to Bobbin; We'll go a-shooting, says Richard to John.
We'll go a-shooting, says John all alone; We'll go a-shooting, says every one.

XMAS GIFTS. The first day of X:mas My mother sent to me A partridge in a pear tree.

YULE DAYS. The king sent his lady on the first Yule day, A popinjay-aye; Who learns my carol & carries it away?

ZOOLOGICAL Gardens, where you shall go too; But it's through A.B.C. that we get to the Zoo.

·WALTER CRANE'S·
·PICTURE BOOKS·

KING·
·LUCKIE·
=BOY'S·
·PARTY·

KING LUCKIEBOY sat in his lofty state chair,
His Chancellor by him,
Attendants, too, nigh him,
For he was expecting some company there.
And Tempus, the footman, to usher them in,
At the drawing-room floor;
And a knock at the door
Came just at the hour they'd announced to begin.

'Twas General Janus, the first to arrive,
In snow-shoes and gaiters,
Escorted by skaters,
And looking quite blue with the cold of his drive,
See him come in, with his footman Aquarius,
Who presents his Ah-kishes,
That's to say, his best wishes,
A choice of fresh colds, and compliments various

63

Friend February was the next
to appear,
With Valentine Day,
Who had plenty to say;
The Fishes in silver to bring
up the rear.

Mr. March was the next, with
Mr. March Hare;
And they, both together,
Remark'd on the weather,
And carried themselves with a
very high air.

Arch April came after, with
bow and with smile;
And—"If they'd allow her,
Miss Sunshiny Shower,"
Arrayed like a sunbeam, in
elegant style.

But ere the King Luckieboy's
best bow begins,
Enters beautiful May,
With a nose-and-a-gay,
And a train which was borne
by two little twins.

Then Madame June's crab, too,
draws up at the door,
And she brought a new moon,
And a plate and a spoon,
With strawberries enough for
the party, and more.

July next, a traveller under the
    sun,
  With a blue and white sky on,
  Brings in a live Lion,
And by none of them there
    could he be outshone.

Till August arrived, who
    brought a young lady,
  And a face so sunburn'd,
  That wherever he turn'd,
Everyone long'd for a place
    that was shady.

67

He was follow'd by one whose
name's in a line
No doubt you remember
His name is September,
Like John Gilpin balanced by
bottles of wine.

"Room, by your leave!" says
the Scorpion outrider,
For honest October,
Who drest very sober
In russet, and brought in Sir
Barrel de Cider.

November the next, arm-in-
arm with the Archer
Who shot at the froggie;
Miss Rayne Dullan Foggie,
And Mr. Jack Frost in a stick-up
and starcher.

December came last, and he
seem'd very old,
And he rode on a goat,
In a very thick coat,
Sprinkled over with snow, and
looking so cold.

But he had brought with him
a green Christmas-tree,
And sprigs of crisp holly,
And all that was jolly
In puddings and presents, as
there you may see.

———————

Now, if this party is such as
may please one,
We hope you'll receive them,
For here we must leave them,
Wishing you all the good things
of the season.

· THE ·

THREE
BEARS

THE THREE BEARS

SOME time ago, ere we were born or thought of,
There lived a little girl, who liked to roam
Through lonely woods and lanes, unknown,
    unsought of
  Such folk who like to stop and stay at home.
She found out curious things in all her travel,
  And one of her adventures I will tell:
Once, in a wood she saw a path of gravel,
  Which led to a small cottage in a dell.

And, as the door stood open, in walked boldly,
 This child, whose name was Silverlocks, I'm told;
There was nobody there to treat her coldly,
 No friend to call her back, no nurse to scold.
She found herself within a parlour charming;
 And there upon the table there were placed
Three basins, sending up a smell so warming,
 That she at once felt hungry, and must taste.
The largest basin first, but hot and biting
 The soup was in it, and the second too;
The smallest basin tasted so inviting,
 That up she ate it all, with small ado.

And next she saw three chairs, and tried to sit in
    The biggest, but it was too hard and high;
The middle one she scarcely seemed to fit in,
    But in the smallest chair sat easily;
And rocked herself, her ease and comfort taking,
    Singing the pretty songs she knew so well;
When, oh! the little chair cracked loud, and,
        breaking,
    Gave way all suddenly, and down she fell.

"Ah, well," she thought, "there may be beds to lie on
   Upstairs; I think I'll go at once and see."
And so there were; she said aloud, "I'll try one,
   For I am tired and sleepy as can be."
The biggest bed was not of feathers, surely,
   It was so hard; and so she tried the next,
And found it little better; but securely
   She slept upon the smallest one, unvext.
The little house belonged to bears, not persons;
                  The Father Bear, so very
               rough and large;
                  The Mother Bear (I have know
                  many worse ones);

And then the little Cub, their only charge.
ey had gone for a walk before their dinner;
Returning, Father growled, "Who's touched my soup?"
ho's touched my soup?" said Mother, with voice thinner;
"But mine," said little Cub, "is finished up!"
ey turned to draw their chairs a little nearer;
'Who's sat in my chair?" growled the Father Bear;
ho's sat in my chair?"
d the Mother, clearer;
And squeaked the little
b,
ho's broken my small
ir?"

77

They rushed upstairs, and Father Bruin,
    growling,
Cried out, "Who's lain upon my bed?"
"Who's lain on mine?" cried Mother
    Bruin, howling;

"But some one *lies* on mine!" the small
       Bear said.
"We'll kill the child, and eat her for our
       dinner,"
The Father growled; but said the Mother,
       "No;
For supper she shall be, and I will skin her."
"No," said the little Cub, "we'll let her go."

So Silverlocks, in sudden terror flying,
Reached home; and when the Nurse the
    story hears,
She says, "You are in luck, there's no
    denying,
To get away in safety from

THREE BEARS."

WALTER·CRANE'S·PICTURE·BOOKS·
BLUEBEARD

BLUEBEARD

ONCE on a time there lived a man
    hated by all he knew,
Both that his ways were very bad,
    and that his beard was blue;
But as he was so rich and grand, and
    led a merry life,
A lady he contrived at last to induce
    to be his wife.

For a month after the wedding they
    lived and had good cheer,
And then said Bluebeard to his wife,
    "I'll say good-bye, my dear;
"Indeed, it is but for six weeks that I
    shall be away,
"I beg that you'll invite your friends,
    and feast and dance and play;
"And all property I'll leave confided
    to your care:
"Here are the keys of all my chests,
    there's plenty and to spare.

"But this small key belongs to one small
    room on the ground floor,—
"And this you must not open, or you
    will repent it sore."
And so he went; and all the friends
    came there from far and wide,
And in her wealth the lady took much
    happiness and pride;
But in a while this kind of joy grew
    nearly satisfied,

And oft she saw the closet door, and longed
    to look inside,
At last she could no more refrain, and turned
    the little key,
And looked within, and fainted straight the
    horrid sight to see;
For there upon the floor was blood, and on
    the walls were wives,
For Bluebeard first had married them, then
    cut their throats with knives.

And this poor wife, distracted, picked the key
    up from the floor,
All stained with blood; and with much fear
    she shut and locked the door.
She tried in vain to clean the key and wash
    the stain away
With sand and soap,—it was no use. Bluebeard
    came back that day;
At once he asked her for the key,—he saw
    the bloody stain,—

"You have been in the closet once,
    and you shall go again!"
"O spare me, spare me! give me
    time, nor kill me hastily!"
"You have a quarter of an hour,—
    then, madam, you must die!"
"O sister Anne, go up, go up, and
    look out from the tower;
"I'm dead unless my brothers come
    in a quarter of an hour!"
And Anne looked once, and Anne
    looked twice, and nothing saw
    abroad,
But shining sun and growing grass,
    and dust upon the road.

"Come down!" cried Bluebeard, "time is
    up!" With many a sigh and moan,
She prayed him for a minute more; he
    shouted still, "Come down!"
"O sister Anne, look out, look out! and do
    you nothing see?"
"At last I see our brothers two come riding
    hastily."
"Now spare me, Bluebeard,—spare thy
    wife!" but as the words were said,

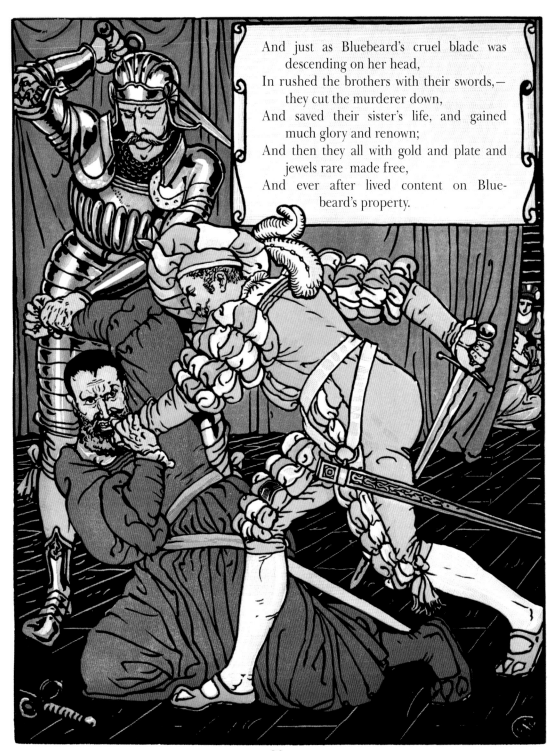

And just as Bluebeard's cruel blade was
    descending on her head,
In rushed the brothers with their swords,—
    they cut the murderer down,
And saved their sister's life, and gained
    much glory and renown;
And then they all with gold and plate and
    jewels rare made free,
And ever after lived content on Blue-
    beard's property.

·WALTER·CRANE'S·
·PICTURE·BOOKS·

·MOTHER·
·HUBBARD.

OLD Mother Hubbard
 Went to her cupboard
To get her poor Dog a bone;
 But when she came there
 The cupboard was bare,
And so the poor Dog had none.

She went to the baker's
    To buy him some bread,
But when she came back,
    The poor Dog was dead.

She went to the joiner's
    To buy him a coffin,
But when she came back,
    The poor Dog was laughing.

She took a clean dish
    To get him some tripe,
But when she came back,
    He was smoking a pipe.

She went to the ale-house
    To get him some beer,
But when she came back,
    The Dog sat in a chair.

95

She went to the tavern
   For white wine and red
But when she came back,
   The Dog stood on his he[a]

She went to the hatter's,
   To buy him a hat,
But when she came back,
   He was feeding the cat.

She went to the barber's
    To buy him a wig,
But when she came back,
    He was dancing a jig.

She went to the fruiterer's
    To buy him some fruit,
But when she came back,
    He was playing the flute.

She went to the tailor's
  To buy him a coat,
But when she came back,
  He was riding a goat.

She went to the cobbler's
  To buy him some shoes,
But when she came back,
  He was reading the news.

She went to the sempstress
  To buy him some linen,
But when she came back,
  The Dog was a-spinning.

She went to the hosier's
  To buy him some hose,
But when she came back,
  He was drest in his clothes.

The Dame made a curtsey,
  The Dog made a bow;
The Dame said,
  "Your servant,"
    The Dog said, "Bow wow!"

This wonderful Dog
  Was Dame Hubbard's delight,
He could sing, he could dance,
  He could read, he could write.

She gave him rich dainties
  Whenever he fed,
And erected a monument
  When he was dead.

VALENTINE
AND ORSON

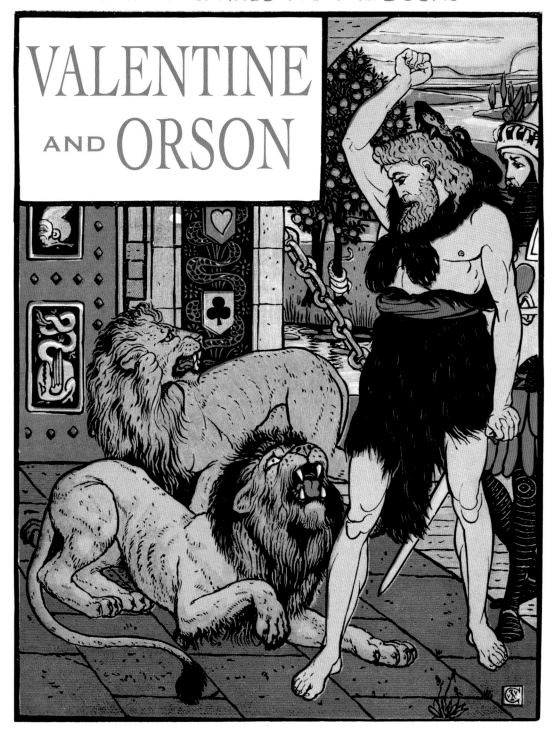

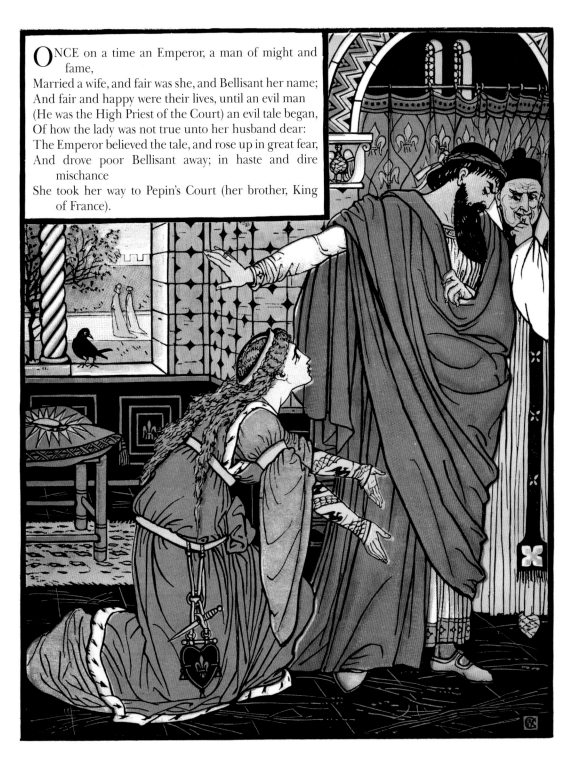

ONCE on a time an Emperor, a man of might and
    fame,
Married a wife, and fair was she, and Bellisant her name;
And fair and happy were their lives, until an evil man
(He was the High Priest of the Court) an evil tale began,
Of how the lady was not true unto her husband dear:
The Emperor believed the tale, and rose up in great fear,
And drove poor Bellisant away; in haste and dire
    mischance
She took her way to Pepin's Court (her brother, King
    of France).

And as she fled, weighed down by grief and sense
    of cruel scorn,
Lo, in the forest two fair sons to Bellisant were born;
But while her servant went to buy some food, a
    great she-bear
Came up, and carried off one child unto her distant
    lair.
Poor Bellisant ran after her, with many a sigh and
    moan;
In vain,—and when she turned again, the other
    child was gone!

Now, Pepin chanced that very day to hunt with all his train
In that same wood, and found the child ere she came back again;
And took him home, and brought him up, and gave him all things fine—
Apparel, horses, and a name,—so he was VALENTINE.
And brave and fair he grew,—King Pepin's daughter loved him well;
The sons were jealous. Now will I his brother's story tell.

105

The she-bear and her savage cu
And nursed him well, and ten
They called him ORSON; in the wo
And all he fought he killed v
Was made by Pepin's sons for gett
Whom they induced to fight v
But Valentine was conqueror,
And served and followed him alv

saved the child alive,
,—well did he grow and thrive,
ived, a strong wild man,
; and so a wicked plan
of Valentine,
, by flattering words and fine.
on owned his might,
they were squire and knight.

Now, in that land there dwelt a man, the
    Green Knight he was called,
Who by his strength and magic arts a lady
    fair enthralled,
And kept in prison dark and strong, and
    none could set her free;
Not even Valentine prevailed, with all his
    bravery.

But Orson threw the Green Knight down,
    and bound him with a chain,
And set the lady free; both brothers then
    start off to gain
The Green Knight's castle-gates,—two roaring
    lions kept guard there,
But down they crouched when they beheld
    the brothers void of fear.

And there within the castle hall they saw a head of brass,
That uttered marvels,—of their birth, and how it came
    to pass;
How in a convent lonely was their mother Bellisant;
How the King and Queen of France were their uncle
    and their aunt;
How the High Priest had confessed his lies, with many
    tears and groans;
How the Emperor, their father, was in search of wife and
    sons.
So the lost were found, the wrong made right, by all
    good rule and line;
They married well, and lived long years—ORSON and
    VALENTINE.

WALTER·CRANE'S·
·PICTURE·BOOKS·

:CINDER·
·ELLA:

THERE was an honest gentleman, who had a daughter dear;
    His wife was dead, he took instead a new one in a year;
She had two daughters—Caroline and Bella were their names;
They called the other daughter Cinderella, to their shames,
Because she had to clean the hearths and black-lead all the
    grates;
She also had to scrub the floors, and wash the dinner plates.
But though the others went abroad, did nothing, smiled, and
    drest,
Yet Cinderella all the time was prettiest and best.
The King who ruled in that country, he had an only son,
Who gave a ball to all the town, when he was twenty-one;
And Caroline and Bella were invited, and they said,
"Cinderella shall leave scrubbing, and act as ladies' maid."

They dressed themselves so fine in silks, and pearls, and
    flowers, and lace.
Poor Cinderella hadn't time to wash her pretty face.
When they started for the ball, full of haughtiness and pride,
Poor Cinderella felt quite sad, and sat her down and cried.
She had not cried much longer than a quarter of an hour,
When a wonderful bright creature appeared upon the floor,
Looked compassionately on her, and said in accents mild,
"I am your Fairy Godmother, so cry no more, my child:
I know that you are sad, and that your sisters are unkind:
Now go and fetch for me the largest pumpkin you can find."
She went and fetched the pumpkin, and the Fairy shook her
    wand,
And changed it to a splendid coach, with cushions rich and
    grand.

Now fetch the mouse-trap from the shelf—there are six
    mice inside;"
She changed them to six prancing steeds, all harnessed
    side by side.
"Now fetch the rat-trap," and there was therein a large
    black rat,
So he was made the coachman, with silk stockings and
    cocked hat.
Six lizards happening to be there, all ready to the hand,
Were changed to powdered footmen, staff and bouquet
    all so grand.
"Now, Cinderella, here's your coach to take you to the
    ball."
"Not as I am," she cried; "like this I cannot go at all."

115

And then the Fairy raised her wand, and touched the shabby
        gown—
It turned to satin, trimmed with lace, and jewels, and swans-
        down.
Her face was clean, her gloves were new, her hair was nicely
        curled,
And on her feet were shoes of glass, the neatest in the world.
"Now, Cinderella, you may go; but take care to return
Before the clock strikes twelve, or else you'll see your carriage
        turn
Into a pumpkin once again, your horses into mice;
Your coachman, footmen, will become rat, lizards, in a trice,
And you yourself, the cinder-girl, will once again become;
So mind that when the clock strikes twelve you must be safe
        at home."

116

She promised, and with joyful heart she gained the palace
    hall,
And danced, and laughed, and looked indeed the fairest of
    them all.
The King's son danced with her, and praised her lovely shape
    and air;
All treated her as if she were the greatest lady there;
But in good time she slipped away, and waited safe at home,
In kitchen corner sitting till her sisters back should come;
And when they came they told her all about the stranger fair,
And what she wore, and how she looked, and how she did
    her hair.
Next night another ball was held—the sisters dressed, and
    went,
And pretty Cinderella, too, by Godmother was sent.

117

The Prince danced with her every dance, and praised her
        more and more,
And laughed and talked so much, that when the clock 'gan
        strike the hour—
The fatal hour of twelve—it took her greatly by surprise;
She turned and fled so quick before the Prince's wondering
        eyes,
That in her haste to reach her coach she dropped her crystal
        shoe;
She had no time to pick it up, as towards home she flew.
The sisters later home returned, and told her all they knew
About the lady and the Prince, and all of it was true.
As Cinderella heard them talk, she turned away her head,
Nor said a word that might not fit her place of kitchen-maid.

Next day was proclamation made: "Whereas, a crystal shoe
Has been discovered at the ball, who is the owner—who?
All ladies now must try it on; the Prince will marry her,
Whoe'er it be, who easily the crystal shoe can wear."
No foot was found to fit the shoe; they tried throughout the
     town;
At last they came unto this house, and called the ladies down.
The sisters try to get it on, and pull, and push, and squeeze,
When Cinderella calmly said, "Allow me, if you please."
The sisters scorned her for the thought, and much surprise
     they knew,
When Cinderella from her pocket pulled the fellow shoe.
She tried them on—they fit—and she, no longer kitchen-maid,
Stands up to meet the Prince in all her beauty fair arrayed.

Now do the sisters kneel, and beg forgiveness for their pride;
And she is kind, as well becomes a noble Prince's bride.
The wedding was most grand, and when they started on
    their tour,
The King and Queen and all the court were standing round
    the door;
And, wishing that for them all happy things might come to
    pass,
They all threw after them for luck old slippers—not of
    glass.
The sisters, full of envy, are reported to have said,
"We'll work ourselves, and never have another kitchen-maid.
We have been idle all our lives,—we'll try another way,
And be industrious instead—it really seems to pay."

THE WALTER CRANE STORYBOOK COLLECTION

Printed and Bound in China by RR Donnelley.
Composed in Baskerville Cyrillic LT Std.

Printed on 157 gsm Chinese matte art paper.
Bound in JHT cloth.

DISTRIBUTED BY DOVER PUBLICATIONS, INC.